Trine, Greg,author.
Goldilocks, private eye

2019
33305242944274
ca   10/01/19

D0445027

Goldilocks
Private Eye

Greg Trine

Art by Ira Baykovska

Malamute Press

San Buenaventura, California

2019

Text copyright © 2019 by Greg Trine
Illustrations copyright © 2019 by Ira Baykovska
All rights reserved.

Malamute Press
San Buenaventura, California

Goldilocks, Private Eye

Names: Trine, Greg, author. | Baykovska, Ira, illustrator.
Title: Goldilocks private eye / Greg Trine ; art by Ira Baykovska.
Description: San Buenaventura, CA: Malamute Press, 2019.
Summary: Goldilocks inherits a failing detective agency and struggles to make it work, encountering massive spiders, enormous bears... and making a friend along the way.
Identifiers: ISBN 978-1-733-95892-9
Publisher's Cataloging-in-Publication Data
Subjects: LCSH Goldilocks and the three bears--Adaptations--Juvenile fiction. | Child detectives--Juvenile fiction. | Friendship--Juvenile fiction. | Humorous stories. | Mystery and detective stories. | Detective and mystery fiction. | CYAC Goldilocks and the three bears--Adaptations--Fiction. | Child detectives--Fiction. | Friendship--Fiction. | BISAC JUVENILE FICTION / Mysteries & Detective Stories.
Classification: LCC PZ7.T7356 Gol 2019 | DDC [Fic]--dc23
Library of Congress Control Number: 2019904271

For Juanita,
the one and only

A Strange Turn of Events

This story was originally written down by my Polish Great Aunt Edna, who then stuffed it into a glass bottle and tossed it into the sea. The bottle later shattered on the rocky shore of a far-away island. But fortunately the story survived. It was snatched up by a passing albatross, who deposited it at my door one day in late October. So if there are holes in the story, dear reader, please blame the albatross.

~ G. T.

Chapter 1

The Girl With the Golden Hair

When her father died, Goldilocks inherited the family business. Her father was a private detective, and Goldilocks got one magnifying glass, three boxes of paper clips, and a trench coat that didn't fit. There was just enough money in the bank to change the name on the door. It now read:

Goldilocks, Private Eye

But Goldilocks didn't know the first thing about being a detective. And her father wasn't exactly the perfect example. But she was pretty sure she knew what a private eye was supposed to *look* like. So she put one baseball cap on backward and another baseball cap on forward and waited for the phone to ring.

Only the phone didn't ring. It just sat there on the desk like a phone with a busted ringer. The phone, by the way, was in perfect working condition. It just wasn't ringing.

Three days went by. Not a peep.

Goldilocks looked across the room at her cat Charlotte. "What do you think, Charlotte?" she asked.

Charlotte didn't respond. She was, after all, a cat. She couldn't form human words. The best she could muster was a tiny *meow*.

Goldilocks knew her cat was incapable of human speech. It was just her way of thinking out loud. Goldilocks, that is, not the cat.

"We have no money and the phone's not ringing. What are we going to do?"

Meow.

The cat was sitting on the windowsill looking at Goldilocks as she paced back and forth.

"No money means no food, Charlotte. No money means no electricity.

It means no heating. It means we can't pay the rent." She went over to the phone and gave it a nudge. "Are you hearing this, phone? Are you?"

The phone just sat there…quietly.

Goldilocks' shoulders sagged. She flopped on the couch and looked over at her cat. "Any ideas, Charlotte? I mean, we're in this together. If I starve, you starve. If I freeze, you freeze. If I get tossed out onto the street, so do you. If I—"

Someone banged on the door.

Goldilocks jumped to her feet. Maybe the phone didn't have to ring. A knock on the door was even better.

"Ha! Charlotte, say hello to our first customer." She crossed the room and opened the door.

It was not a customer at all. It was the landlady, Mrs. Vanderflip. She wore overalls and a tool belt. A dingy ball cap held her gray hair in place. And she wasn't smiling. She stepped into the room waving a piece of paper. "Three months, young lady. You owe me three months rent. If you don't pay up, guess what happens to you"—she turned toward the window—"and your cat?"

"Uh—" Goldilocks was pretty sure she knew what would happen. But she couldn't get the words out, not with a raging landlady right in front of her.

"I'll tell you what happens." Mrs. Vanderflip's tool belt rattled as she spoke. So did her double chins. Or maybe they just wobbled. She put her hands on her hips and bent at the waist, leaning toward Goldilocks until their noses practically touched. "Eviction, young lady. You'll be out in the street. That's what will happen. What do you have to say about that?"

Goldilocks didn't know what to say, other than, "Uh…my father just died?" she said quietly. Maybe a little sympathy was in order, she thought. After all, her father was dead, and she was just a ten-year-old kid.

"I don't want to hear it," Mrs. Vanderflip said. "Pay up or you're out of here!" Then she walked away, slamming the door behind her.

The Goldilocks Detective Agency office was attached to a small apartment. This is where she and her father had lived. Being tossed out of the office also meant being tossed out of her home.

Out onto the street.

Out into the cold.

Huge tears rolled down her cheeks. She looked across the room at her cat. "What are we going to do, Charlotte?" She asked.

But Charlotte wasn't listening. She was looking out the window, watching a wagon with bars on the windows moving down the street. It was pulled by a black horse and led by a wild-haired man with a scowl on his face and a gleam in his eye.

"Charlotte?" Goldilocks snapped her fingers, trying to get her cat's attention.

Charlotte didn't notice. She kept staring down at the man and his cart. There was something about him.

Something that made her fur stand up.

Chapter 2

Goldilocks' Big Idea

The town was called Lick Skillet and it sat up against the Black Forest—though the trees were mostly green. The forest was so deep and so dark that only the extremely brave or extremely foolish dared enter. Who knew what kind of wild animals lived in such a place? Or what kind of reptiles? Legend had it that the spiders were so big that they left footprints.

Just a legend, of course, but still.

It was the place of nightmares for every kid in Lick Skillet. At least once a week, Goldilocks had a bad dream about the Black Forest and its ferocious beasts and enormous spiders.

But at least the town itself was safe. As long as you stayed clear of the Black Forest, you had nothing to worry about. This was Goldilocks' life-long plan—stay away from the Black Forest and all would be well.

Goldilocks went to the window to see what Charlotte was staring at. Down below, on the street, the man with the scowl on his face and the gleam in his eye walked beside his horse, scanning the street for his next victim. He worked for the orphanage outside of town. If you were a kid without parents, watch out!

Sometimes he even snatched kids who *had* parents.

He was that kind of kid-snatcher.

His horse pulled the Patty Wagon, which was named after his last captive. Before that it was called the Henry Wagon, which came after the Thomas Wagon. With any luck he'd soon change the name to the Goldie Wagon. He'd heard rumors. There was a girl with golden curls, and she was all alone.

Goldilocks stepped back from the window. A chill ran up her spine. She wanted no part of the crazy man and his Patty Wagon. She also knew that the only way to stay out of his evil clutches was to stay off the street.

And the only way to do that was to pay the rent.

"Charlotte," she said, "we've got to get this detective agency up and running again."

Not that it was ever really up and running. Not when her father was in charge.

"Dad didn't know what he was doing," Goldilocks said, still thinking out loud. She paced back and forth in front of her cat. "We just need to—"

We just need to what? she asked herself. That was the question. What to do? How to make the Goldilocks Detective Agency successful enough to pay the bills?

"We just need to—" she said again, but didn't have the answer. She had no idea where to begin.

She sat down on the couch, absently picked up the remote, and turned on the television. It was a commercial about bathroom cleaner.

"We just need to advertise!" Goldilocks yelled, jumping to her feet. She pointed to the television. "That's how it's done, Charlotte. Customers aren't calling because they don't know we're here. We need to get the word out!"

She went to her computer and began working on a flyer. In big black letters she typed:

Goldilocks Detective Agency

Then she got to thinking...what is it that detective agencies do? What services do they provide? Charlotte crossed the room and jumped up on the desk. She sniffed at the computer and gave a tiny *meow*.

"My thoughts exactly, Charlotte," Goldilocks said. Not that she knew what her cat was saying. When Charlotte said meow, she probably meant something like...*meow*.

Still, Goldilocks had some ideas of her own. Below Goldilocks Detective Agency, she wrote:

Solver of Mysteries

Missing Persons

"What else, Charlotte?"

Meow.

"Perfect." Below Missing Persons, Goldilocks added one final item:

General Crime Fighting

Then she listed her phone number and address and printed twenty copies. She grabbed her coat and was about to head out the door, when she stopped herself. What about that scary man and his Patty Wagon? Did he know there was a golden-haired girl who had recently lost her father?

Just in case, Goldilocks removed her two baseball caps. Then she grabbed a knitted hat and put in on, stuffing her hair inside.

Golden curls? What golden curls? She was just a kid with a hat.

She turned to her cat, who was still sitting on the desk inspecting the computer monitor. "Charlotte, you're in charge. If anyone calls, take a message."

Then she went out, locking the door behind her.

Chapter 3

The Wild-Haired Man

"The rent, young lady, the rent!" It was Mrs. Vanderflip and her rattling tool belt. She was standing on a stepladder at the end of the hall, replacing a light bulb. "I'd feel guilty if I had to toss you out on the street."

Goldilocks said nothing as she scooted around the stepladder and started down the stairs.

"But I'd get over it, young lady. I promise you. I'd get over it!"

Goldilocks stopped and looked up. "You'll get your money, Mrs. Vanderflip. I have a plan."

"That's exactly what your father used to tell me. He always had a plan."

Goldilocks didn't say anything more. She didn't want to argue about the merits of her plan. She was much more interested in *doing* the plan. And right now the plan was to get the word out about the Goldilocks Detective Agency. Once people knew she was there, the work would come rolling in. Work rolling in meant money rolling in and money rolling in meant she could pay the rent.

She stepped out onto the street and was surprised by how the wind had picked up. Holding the flyers tightly against her chest, she walked up to a streetlight and taped one of the flyers to it, adding extra tape to keep it from blowing away. Then she stepped back and read it.

Goldilocks Detective Agency

Solver of Mysteries

Missing Persons

General Crime Fighting

473 Main Street, Lick Skillet, 555-4782

She wasn't sure if detectives also fought crime. Then again, she really wanted her phone to ring. Maybe adding extra services was a good thing. Plus, she had to fill the flyer. Solver of Mysteries and Missing Persons and nothing more left too much white space. Adding the extra line—and extra service—balanced it out.

"I'm a mystery solver *and* a crime fighter," she said out loud.

Then she walked down the street to the Laundromat and tacked a flyer to the bulletin board inside. Next she went to the library and did the same. This was followed by more streetlights.

She walked all over town, taping and tacking up flyers, getting the word out. Everyone had a mystery to solve, didn't they?

Up one street and down another. And the more Goldilocks walked, the windier it became, until suddenly—

Woosh!

Off came her hat.

Out tumbled her golden curls.

Goldilocks had forgotten she had been wearing a hat. But no matter, she taped up her last flyer. Then she stepped back and nodded. "That ought to do it. Looks good if I do say so—"

"You!" It was the wild-haired man with the smirk and the gleam. His face was still smirking! His eyes were still gleaming! He was a block away, pointing a finger. Then he grabbed a giant net from the top of the Patty Wagon. "You with the golden hair, don't move!"

Oh no! she said to herself. *He's seen my curls. I knew these locks would get me into trouble some day.*

Goldilocks sprinted down the block, fear rising inside her. She'd heard stories about the orphanage. Terrible stories. Nightmares. Worse than the Black Forest and its horrible beasts. Worse than giant spiders.

She shot down a narrow side street, then another. Behind her the wild-haired man kept coming, matching her turn for turn. She could hear the hooves of the black horse clopping on the pavement, the wild man yelling, "Give it up, Girlie."

Goldilocks wasn't about to give up anything. She rounded the corner onto Main Street and practically threw herself through the open door of her building.

Mrs. Vanderflip was there, sweeping the hall. "Rent—" she started to say before Goldilocks shushed her.

"There's a man outside, Mrs. Vanderflip," she said, gasping for breath. "If he catches me, you won't get your rent." Then she ran up the stairs to her office/apartment and locked herself in.

"Charlotte," she said, still breathing hard, "I'm in trouble."

Charlotte was looking out the window at the wild-haired man and a black horse pulling a cart. Just as before, her fur stood up.

"Do you see him, Charlotte? Is he out there?"

Meow.

Goldilocks couldn't bring herself to look out the window. She stood there in the middle of the room, trying to calm herself.

When her breathing got back to normal she said, "That was a close one, Charlotte. That was very, very close."

She let out a long sigh. Charlotte walked over, purring as she rubbed against Goldilocks' legs.

And then someone knocked on the door.

Chapter 4

The Knock on the Door

"What have you done, Mrs. Vanderflip?" Goldilocks glanced down at her cat. "She turned us in, Charlotte. The landlady turned us in."

Charlotte stopped rubbing against Goldilocks' ankles and looked up.

"What was she thinking?" Goldilocks said. "I can't very well pay the rent if I'm locked in an orphanage."

The knock came again.

Goldilocks went to the door and looked out through the peephole.

But it wasn't the wild-haired man. It was the normal-haired variety. In fact, this guy was perfectly groomed and was wearing a suit and tie. No smirk at all…not even a gleam.

"Uh…" Goldilocks stammered. "Who's there?"

"Is this the Goldilocks Detective Agency?" said the man. "It says so on the door."

"It is."

"Well, let me in. I have a case to discuss."

Goldilocks looked at her cat and smiled. "Did you hear that, Charlotte? A case. An honest-to-goodness case." All kinds of things popped into her head at once. A case meant rent money. It meant not being tossed out onto the street. It meant not being captured by a wild-haired man and having his wagon named after her. And it certainly meant not being locked in an orphanage.

She opened the door.

The man stepped into the office and Goldilocks peered down the hall. No sign of the wild-haired man. Good. She closed the door and turned to her customer.

"What kind of case?" Goldilocks asked. She saw that the man was holding one of her flyers. His hair was black as tar and parted down the middle. His mustache was so thin, it looked like he'd drawn it on with a felt pen.

He looked at the flyer and said, "Missing persons. Is that one of your specialties?"

Goldilocks sat in the chair in front of her desk and gestured for the man to take a seat on the other side. It seemed like the right move. She'd seen it a thousand times in movies. She'd have offered him a cigar if she had any.

Instead, she simply nodded and tried to act like she knew what she was doing. "Missing persons? Absolutely. It's what I do." She leaned forward. "Tell me more, Mr...."

"Sims. Frank Sims. It's my grandparents. They're missing."

Goldilocks grabbed a pad of paper and began taking notes. This was also something she'd seen in movies. "Go on."

"It's the strangest thing," the man said. "I went to see my grandparents the other day. They're my only living grandparents. And I'm their only grandson who lives close enough to visit. So I check up on them periodically. It's my duty—it's what grandsons do."

"I understand."

"But when I got there, there was no sign of them. And someone else was there."

"Someone else?"

"Yes, Miss Goldilocks." The man stood up and placed his hands on the desk. He leaned in. "Bears are living in my grandparents house."

The pencil slipped from Goldilocks's hand. "Come again?"

"You heard me. My grandparents are missing and bears have taken their place. Walking on two legs—like they're human or something. Sitting in chairs, using the beds, eating out of bowls. Have you ever heard of such a thing?"

This being her very first case, Goldilocks hadn't heard much of anything.

She shook her head. "Never."

"I'll pay whatever you like. Just find my grandparents." He pulled a business card from his front pocket and placed it on the desk. "You can reach me at this number."

"Where do your grandparents live?"

"In the Black Forest, of course."

Goldilocks gasped. She felt like she was about to faint and grabbed hold of the desk to steady herself. *Black Forest? What about the beasts? What about the spiders?*

"Is there a problem?" the man asked.

Problem? Yes, there was a problem. The Black Forest was a very big problem. Hadn't he heard the stories? The creatures? The spiders? After all, only the extremely brave or extremely foolish dared enter the Black Forest. And Goldilocks was neither.

"Uh…no problem at all," she lied. A huge lie…a whopper. She desperately needed the case because she desperately needed the rent money. Plus, it would be nice to be able to eat now and then. But the Black Forest? Really? Did it have to be the Black Forest? Couldn't it be something more like Maple Street?...or South Jennings Avenue?

"Good," said the man, turning to leave. "Take the trail that runs past the orphanage. You can't miss the house. Yellow with white trim."

Great. Black Forest AND orphanage. All in the same case? Was this some kind of joke?

Goldilocks kept holding onto the desk, still feeling like she was about to keel over any second.

The man started toward the door, then turned back. "Oh, and it's best if you stay on the trail. It's pretty easy to lose your way if you leave the trail."

After the man left, Goldilocks sagged in her chair. She looked over at Charlotte, who had climbed back onto the windowsill and was looking out at the street.

"What are we going to do, Charlotte?"

Meow.

What *could* she do? She had already agreed to the case. People were missing and she was a missing people finder, wasn't she?

Chapter 5

The Orphanage Just Outside of Lick Skillet

When the wild-haired man rounded the corner onto Main Street, there was no sign of the girl with the golden curls. No sign at all. The man spotted an old woman in a dingy baseball cap and a tool belt around her waist, sweeping out the entrance to a building. He wiped the scowl from his face and approached her.

"Excuse me, but did you see a little girl with golden hair pass this way?"

The woman took one look at the wild-haired man and his Patty Wagon, which had formerly been named the Henry Wagon. She knew immediately who was asking for Goldilocks. This was the notorious Lick Skillet Kid Snatcher. He imprisoned children for a living. Why should she make his job any easier?

Best to ignore the man, she thought. She lowered her head and kept sweeping.

The man persisted. "Ma'am? Did you see her? It's really important that I find her."

The old woman huffed. *Important? Why? So you can change the name of your wagon? The Goldie Wagon did have a ring to it, but still.*

"Ma'am?"

"I saw no one," she said finally.

"She just came around that corner. You had to have seen something." The scowl was starting to creep back onto his face. He wiped it off again and smiled. "Just a few seconds ago, you couldn't have missed her."

"Fine." The lady pointed down the street with her broom handle. "She went that way. Better hurry. She was running like the dickens."

"Much obliged, Ma'am." He set off down the street, and now, with his back toward the woman, he let the scowl return in all its scowliness. The gleam in his eye came back too.

"Where are you, little girl?" he snarled under his breath.

But the girl with the golden curls was nowhere to be seen. It was as if she had vanished into thin air. She'd rounded the corner and was gone.

He searched up and down the streets and through the back alleys of Lick Skillet, but there was no sign of her.

Even though the Patty Wagon had no captive, the horse panted. It had been a long day of kid-hunting. As the sun dipped toward the horizon, the wild-haired man called it a day. He gave up the search and returned to the orphanage.

I'll get her tomorrow, he said to himself. With any luck, the Patty Wagon would soon have a new name.

At least now he knew the rumors of the girl with the golden curls were true. She was an orphan, all right—she wouldn't have run if she wasn't—and orphans belonged at the orphanage.

Just outside the town of Lick Skillet sat the orphanage. It was called The Orphanage Just Outside of Lick Skillet. Not the most interesting name in the world, but the building was one scary place. No wonder the wild-haired man had a permanent scowl. You would too if you lived and worked at The Orphanage Just Outside of Lick Skillet. It was an old castle, complete with drawbridge and moat. Hard to get in…and nearly impossible to escape. Not impossible, but nearly so. A month earlier an orphan had escaped and was never seen nor heard from again.

The man and his Patty Wagon pulled to a stop in front of the moat and waited for the drawbridge to drop. Then he went inside. He had barely returned to his room when he was summoned to the director's office.

"Well?" asked the director. "Is it time to change the name of your wagon?" He leaned forward, gazing at the wild-haired man through thick glasses, which made his eyes look frighteningly large. And those large eyes went perfectly with the man himself, who was enormous. His hands were the size of dinner plates.

"Sir?"

"The girl with the golden curls. Wasn't she the one you were after?"

The wild-haired man nodded in disgust. "It was. She's still at large."

"What!" The director's eyes grew even larger. "You know how it works here, Tom. The government pays us based on how many kids we have. More kids means more money for me *and* you."

Tom looked away from his large-eyeballed employer.

"How long has the wagon been named Patty?" asked the director.

"I don't know," Tom said. "A couple of weeks?"

"Months, Tom. It's been months. You can't let this one slip away. Don't make me replace my favorite kid-snatcher."

Tom nodded. "You won't have to, Sir. The golden-haired girl is mine. She just doesn't know it yet."

"Glad to hear it. I'll expect better news tomorrow."

Tom the Kid-Snatcher left the director's office and went back to his room. He lay on his bed and thought back to what had happened on Main Street. One second the girl had been there and the next she was gone. How could she have disappeared like that? She couldn't have, he decided. Not without help.

He sat up suddenly. "That old lady with the tool belt, the one with the broom!" he said out loud. "She knows something."

And if she did know something, he'd get her to tell him. He had ways of getting people to talk.

Chapter 6
Goldilocks on the Case

It was a sleepless night for one golden-haired girl. She tossed and turned, muttering under her covers, "Forest, spiders, and orphanage. Oh my!"

In the morning Goldilocks shuffled to the kitchen, followed by her cat. "The Black Forest, Charlotte," she said with a shudder. She was even afraid of tiny apartment spiders. What was she going to do when she came across the footprint-leaving variety? And what about the other beasts of the forest?

"Not good, Charlotte. Not good at all."

She opened a can of tuna and dumped half of it into Charlotte's bowl. Then she grabbed a fork and ate directly from the can. "I know we need the money, but if I die, who's going to take care of you? Maybe we should hold out for something better. Maybe we'll get another case. An in-town one. No spiders. No beasts."

She took another bite. "Any thoughts, Charlotte?"

Meow.

It was the most pathetic meow Goldilocks had ever heard. Maybe she was just imagining it, but the tiny meow seemed to be saying something like, "Don't look at me. I'm just a tiny furball…and by the way, I'm hungry."

Her cat was hungry. This little creature that depended on her for everything wasn't getting enough food.

Goldilocks didn't need any more motivation than that. She slapped her fork on the counter and gave Charlotte the rest of the tuna. "I'll do it, Charlotte. Black Forest or no Black Forest, beasts or no beasts, spiders or no—*gulp*—spiders, I'm on the case."

She grabbed her school backpack and began loading it up with supplies. Not that she had many supplies, but still. The important stuff went into the bag—magnifying glass, trench coat, paperback copy of *The*

Wind in the Willows. It was her father's favorite story, so of course she had to take it along. Besides, you never know when you might want to stop and read something. Maybe between spider attacks.

Once the bag was packed, Goldilocks slung it over her shoulder and looked down at her cat, who was just finishing the last of the tuna. "Be back soon, Charlotte. You're in charge."

Meow.

"I will. You too." Then she went out, locking the door behind her.

It wasn't until she was halfway to the trailhead that she realized that she had forgotten her hat. Her golden curls were in plain view.

Great, she thought. *Nothing like being conspicuous.*

But there was no turning back. She was almost at the trail. Ahead she could see the ancient castle, otherwise known as The Orphanage Just Outside of Lick Skillet. It was shrouded in a ring of mist rising up from the moat.

When she reached the trail, she followed it along the castle wall. Frogs splashed into the moat as she passed, then croaked at her from the water. Goldilocks kept looking up at the high walls of the orphanage. *What a place*, she thought. *Those poor kids.*

Thinking of the orphan captives made her think of the orphan *capturer*, the wild-haired man, Tom the Kid-Snatcher—she'd heard somewhere that his name was Tom. And this caused her to pick up the pace, leaving the orphanage behind. In front of her stood the Black Forest. In the bright sunlight, Goldilocks was surprised to see how un-scary it looked. *It's just a bunch of trees*, she thought. Birds chirped and flitted among the branches. *Maybe it's not such a bad place after all.*

Just in case, she pulled a wooden spoon from her school backpack and shoved it into her belt. A wooden spoon wasn't the best weapon in the world, but if you hit someone hard enough with it, maybe, just maybe…

Soon she was moving among the trees of the Black Forest.

"Not bad," she said to herself, trying to stay positive, though the birdsongs were suddenly not so sweet.

She twitched at every sound, every rustle of leaves, and she kept listening for footsteps, the kind giant spiders might make.

She didn't hear any spider footsteps. None at all. What she did hear was a galloping horse. She turned around. Coming down the path was the black horse she'd seen the day before. This time it wasn't pulling the Patty Wagon. On its back sat the wild-haired man, Tom the Kid-Snatcher, holding his giant net like a jousting spear.

Through his scowl he yelled out, "I've got you now, girlie!"

Goldilocks turned and ran, her heartbeat jackhammering away.

But she knew there was no outrunning a galloping horse. If she stayed on the path, that is. She'd be captured for sure. She'd be locked away in The Orphanage Just Outside of Lick Skillet. She'd have a wagon named after her.

Her only escape was to leave the path. She hopped a moss-covered log, then another and tore through the ferns and ducked a few low branches. The trees grew so closely together that no sunlight reached the forest floor. Goldilocks looked for the tighter gaps, just big enough for a girl to slip through but too small for a horse to follow. Hopefully.

She kept running.

Deeper into the Black Forest.

Further away from the path.

Chapter 7

The Black Forest

Goldilocks glanced over her shoulder. No sign of the black horse or its rider. There was also no sign of the path. Hadn't her client said something about the dangers of wandering away from the trail? That it was easy to lose your way? She looked around at the dark forest, the fallen trees and the upright ones, the ferns and the moss-covered vines. She'd left the trail, all right. She'd left it in a very big way.

But she had to, didn't she? The alternative was even worse—locked up in an orphanage and a wagon with her name on it.

The Goldie Wagon had a ring to it, but still.

She stopped running and listened. If Tom the Kid-Snatcher was still after her, he had to be on foot. If she heard footsteps, it could be the human *or* spider variety. Either way it would mean one thing. Run!

But she heard nothing. Just the wind through the trees and the occasional squawk of a bird. After a while, she started walking again. Maybe the path zigzagged through the forest and if she kept moving forward she'd bump into it. She still had a case to solve. And there was no solving the case without finding the path that led to the yellow house with white trim. The house with the bears, formerly occupied by her client's grandparents.

All through the day Goldilocks kept moving. She heard no footsteps of any kind, although once she walked right into a giant spider web and thought for sure she was going to be gobbled up by something big and hairy with eight legs. It didn't happen—no spider appeared at all—and she spent the next twenty minutes removing spider web goo from her clothing.

Once she was goo-less, she noticed the darkness of the forest was growing even darker. *Great*, she thought. *Spending the night in the Black Forest.*

You've never seen dark until you've been in the Black Forest at night. The dense trees that block out the sun during the day also block out the stars at night. If there was a moon out, Goldilocks certainly couldn't see it. She also couldn't see her hand in front of her face.

And with the darkness came the cold. Goldilocks dug into her backpack and pulled out a box of matches. *Build a fire*, she told herself. *A little light and a little heat will do a body good. And more than likely, Tom the Kid-Snatcher is miles away.*

That's what she told herself. That she was so deep into the forest that no one would see the light from her fire.

To be on the safe side, though, she kept the fire small. She had only herself to warm and it did put out enough light to make the forest seem a little less scary. Goldilocks relaxed. Once again, she had escaped the clutches of the evil kid-snatcher. Now all she had to do was wait for the sun to rise, and when it did, she'd find the trail—somehow—and get back to work, solving the case of the missing grandparents.

That was the plan anyway.

And then—

Crack!

Was it a footstep? Or did a branch just feel like snapping in two all by itself?

Kick the fire out! she told herself.

But before she could a move, a net came down around her.

"Gotcha!" a voice snarled out of the dark. It was Tom the Kid-Snatcher. "Well, well, the girl with the golden curls. We meet at last."

He lifted the net, grabbed Goldilocks by the arm, and yanked her to her feet.

"Let me go!"

The kid-snatcher pulled her close, firelight illuminating his wild hair. The gleam in his eye. The scowl. "Let you go? Why, I wouldn't think of such a thing. We're just getting to know each other."

He reached into the satchel that hung from his shoulder. "Now where is that rope?"

Goldilocks wriggled and kicked. "Please," she said. "I have a cat. She needs—"

Something whizzed through the night air. A second later a heavy stone fell to the ground, along with the limp body of Tom the Kid-Snatcher. A girl stepped out of the woods and stooped beside him, feeling his neck for a pulse. She looked up at Goldilocks. "He's still breathing. He'll have a headache when he wakes up, but he's alive." Then she stood and grabbed Goldilocks' hand. "Follow me."

Goldilocks stammered, "Who...who are you?"

"The name's Patty," the girl said.

In the dim light from the fire, Goldilocks noticed the girl's shabby clothing, like she had just escaped prison or something. She appeared to be about Goldilocks' age. Her dark hair—possibly red, though it was a little too dark to tell—hung out the back of a baseball cap.

"Patty Wagon Patty?" Goldilocks asked.

"The same. Let's go." She nodded toward Tom the Kid-Snatcher. "He's starting to come out of it."

"I...uh..." Goldilocks stammered again, uncertain.

"Trust me. We need to get out of here now!"

Goldilocks nodded. She'd already felt the iron grip of the kid snatcher once. And once was enough. She grabbed her backpack and kicked out the fire. Then she and Patty Wagon Patty vanished into the trees.

Chapter 8

Patty Wagon Patty

The thing about complete darkness is that your eyes will never adjust. There's nothing to adjust to. Complete absence of light is complete absence of light. Goldilocks was still holding the hand of Patty Wagon Patty, walking in complete darkness, but somehow not tripping.

"Do...do you know where you're going?" Goldilocks stammered, trying not to think about things that creep in the night. Like spiders.

"More or less. But I have a light. Hold on." A second later Patty held up a penlight. The bulb was in her fist so just a small amount of light came through. "It's an old orphanage trick. Enough light to see but not enough to alert the bad guys." She glanced behind her. "And Tom the Kid-Snatcher is as bad as they come."

They kept moving, Patty's tiny light showing the way.

"Old orphanage trick?" Goldilocks asked.

"Yeah, sometimes we'd sneak out after curfew to grab a snack or something. Or sometimes we'd do it just because we could. Sneak out, that is. Thumb our noses at the boss, you know?"

Goldilocks didn't know at all, but she nodded like she understood.

Patty went on. "The Orphanage Just Outside of Lick Skillet." She shivered at the memory. "What a vile place. They have cockroaches the size of my shoes."

"Wow!" Goldilocks was amazed. "The size of your shoes, really?"

"No, not really. But they do have cockroaches. Isn't that bad enough? They ought to shut that place down. Cockroaches, rats, drafty buildings— is that any way to raise kids?"

"No way at all," Goldilocks agreed.

Patty leaned against a fallen tree and let go of Goldilocks' hand. "I'll tell you what, the director and Tom the Kid-Snatcher are lining their pockets with the money they receive from the government. But not much is spent on caring for the orphans."

"That's why you escaped?" Goldilocks had heard the story of the famous orphanage escape, the one-and-only escape. It was legendary. And here was the legend herself.

Patty shrugged. "I'd always done pretty well living on the streets. Never had to deal with cockroaches or rats anyway. So one day I told myself it's time to leave…and I did."

Goldilocks straddled the log, facing her new friend. "But how?" she asked. "The castle wall is a mile high. And the moat?"

"It wasn't easy," Patty said. "I made a rope out of old shirts and dropped over the wall one night."

"And the moat?"

Patty nodded. "Yep, swam the moat. Some of the nastiest water you'll ever see." She shivered with the thought.

"Frogs seemed to like it," Goldilocks said, remembering their splashing and croaking.

"What do they know? Never trust someone who eats flies for a living." Patty hopped over the log. "Let's keep moving. We're almost there."

"Where's there?"

"You'll see." When Goldilocks gave her a worried look, Patty added,

"My place in the woods. My secret hideout. Safe from all manner of kid-snatchers."

"How about giant spiders?"

"The foot-print leaving variety? That's a bedtime story."

"A scary bedtime story," Goldilocks said. "So is your secret hideout a cave?"

"Not exactly."

A few minutes later, after hopping a tiny creek, Patty opened her fist to let more light out. "This is it," she said. In front of them stood a huge slab of rock, ten feet high, and more than twice that in width, and like everything else in the Black Forest, it was covered in moss.

"This is it?" Goldilocks made a face. A rock was her hide out?

"You can't see it? That's good," Patty said. "But watch this." She walked up to the center of the rock and moved some of the moss aside, revealing a wide crack running the entire height of the rock.

Goldilocks' eyes popped. "A secret passage."

Patty moved forward, gesturing. "Follow me."

The crack in the rock zigged and zagged, and after a while Patty took the penlight out of her fist completely. "Isn't that cool?" she said. "The passage is too twisty for light to escape."

"Very cool," Goldilocks agreed.

"And it gets better." After a few more turns, the passage widened to the size of a small room, opened to the sky.

Goldilocks looked up. "Stars!" The first she'd seen all night.

A small pile of coals glowed in the center of the open space. Patty added a few small sticks and branches. Soon the two of them were sitting before a fire.

"I only have a fire at night, when no one will see the smoke."

"Good idea," Goldilocks said. She thought for a moment, then added, "By the way, thanks for the rescue. That orphanage sounds pretty horrible. Glad I didn't have to see it up close and personal."

Patty added another stick to the fire and shrugged. "You're welcome. So what's your story? A girl alone in the Black Forest at night? That's a tale I'd like to hear."

Goldilocks edged closer to the fire, feeling its warmth. "You really want to know, Patty Wagon Patty?"

"I'm all ears."

Chapter 9

Tom the Kid-Snatcher

Tom the Kid-Snatcher awoke to complete darkness. He had no idea where he was, just that it was dark and his head hurt. He reached out a hand and felt the dirt and pine needles of the forest floor. Slowly, it came back to him. The Black Forest, the girl with the golden curls. He'd had her in his grasp when the lights went out.

"What the heck!" he said out loud. A throbbing headache and no sign of the girl with the golden curls.

He stood up and reached into his pocket for a flashlight, something kid-snatchers have at all times. It was part of the kid-snatchers tool kit—for night work. Because being sneaky meant working when no one could see you sneak.

As soon as he turned on the flashlight, he saw the large rock at his feet. The rock with his blood on it.

"So she had help," he said. "The girl with the golden curls…someone came to her rescue."

But who?

Tom the Kid-Snatcher picked up the rock, turning it over in his hand. *Hmm*, he thought, *the size of a baseball. Someone with perfect aim, hurling a rock the size of a baseball meant one person and one person only.*

"Patty Wagon Patty," he said through gritted teeth. He was sure of it. Once, when the orphans challenged the orphanage staff to a baseball game, wasn't it Patty who struck everyone out? Even the director, who'd played college ball, whiffed on three pitches in a row.

Tom tossed the rock aside. "It's Patty all right. If I find her, I'll find the girl with the golden curls."

And vice-versa. Finding the girl with the golden curls meant finding Patty Wagon Patty. Two for one. Wouldn't his boss be happy?

He'd probably get a bonus.

He made his way through the forest and back to his horse, which he had left near the trail where the trees grew too thick to continue on horseback. Then he headed back to the orphanage. He'd eventually return to the Black Forest to resume the hunt for the girl with the golden curls and her rock-throwing companion. But first he needed to get his head checked out. Being knocked unconscious was nothing to take lightly.

And the closer he got to the orphanage, the angrier he became. He'd been hit in the head by a flying rock, hurled like a fastball by a former resident of The Orphanage Just Outside of Lick Skillet. He'd make her pay. He'd make them all pay.

It was a long and painful ride back to the orphanage. When he got there, he roused the kids from their beds.

"Line up!" he shouted. "It's spanking time!"

"What did we do?" the orphan called Henry asked.

"Not a thing." Tom the Kid-Snatcher's snarl was back, along with the gleam in his eye. "I just feel like spanking. Now line up."

Chapter 10

Henry Wagon Henry

Henry, formerly known as Henry Wagon Henry, stirred in his sleep. If you could call it sleep. It's pretty hard to sleep when your rear end is hurting...and Henry's rear end had just been given a beating for no reason at all.

He threw off his covers and grabbed his penlight. Maybe a midnight snack would make him feel better. He put the penlight in his fist and headed out of the boys' dormitory to the common room between the boys' and girls' living areas.

He was not alone. Thomas, formerly known as Thomas Wagon Thomas, was sitting in the common area along with two girls from the girls' dorm.

"Couldn't sleep?" Thomas asked.

"Sore hindquarters?" asked one of the girls.

"You could say that," Henry said. Then he turned off his penlight. Thomas held his in his fist, giving just enough light for the four of them.

One of the girls held out a box of crackers. "Take a load off, Henry. Have a cracker."

Henry sat down and fished a cracker from the box. He glanced at Thomas, who'd been at the orphanage longer than any of them. "Has this ever happened before? The spanking, I mean."

Thomas shook his head. "Uh-uh. Not that I remember. And my butt has a memory like an elephant."

"So does mine," said one of the girls. "It's the first spanking ever."

"Hope it's not a trend," Henry muttered. He could deal with the cockroaches and the occasional rodent, but spanking was a different matter. "If it is, I'm out of here."

"Yeah, good luck with that," Thomas said.

"It's been done before," Henry shot back.

"Once before," Thomas said. "By Patty Wagon Patty, and she was super human. Did you see her fastball?"

Henry nodded. He *had* seen her fastball. Patty Wagon Patty had skills on top of skills. But no one was super human, because real life was not a comic book. If Patty had escaped, so could he.

But for the time being, he said nothing. If spanking was the new trend, he'd make his escape and do so quietly…after everyone was asleep.

And so the foursome munched on crackers and complained about their sore hindquarters. When they couldn't keep their eyes open any longer, they headed back to the dorms.

Henry waited for Thomas' breathing to become slow and steady before he got out of bed. Then he crept to the laundry room and started tying shirts together. *This was how Patty had done it*, he told himself. *A shirt rope.*

And what was good enough for Patty Wagon Patty was good enough for Henry Wagon Henry.

He finished the rope. A few minutes later, he disappeared over the castle wall.

Chapter 11

Patty's Hideout

Goldilocks took a deep breath. Where to start the story? Her father's death? Inheriting a bankrupt detective agency? The wild-haired man and his Patty Wagon? Her almost-eviction? The case of the missing grandparents?

Goldilocks took another deep breath. She decided to start from the beginning, Since she and Patty Wagon Patty had just met, wouldn't she want to know everything? And that meant leaving nothing out.

"Just like you, I'm all alone," Goldilocks began. "When my father died, he left me his detective agency, which wasn't the most successful operation in the world. So I'm behind on the rent and on the verge of getting tossed out onto the street."

Patty shrugged. "Living on the street isn't so bad. Trust me."

"Anyway," Goldilocks continued. "My dad was a good guy, just not a good business guy. He never advertised. How can you run a detective agency if no one knows you're there?

"So I put out some flyers and a man showed up and said his grandparents were missing and bears were living in their house."

Patty's mouth flopped open. "Bears? Did I hear you right? Bears are living in the grandparents' house?"

Goldilocks nodded. "Apparently. That's why I'm in the Black Forest, to investigate, to solve the case of the missing grandparents, and…to collect my fee so I don't get thrown out onto the street and so I can feed my cat." She poked at the fire. "But as you know, Tom the Kid-Snatcher has a nose for kids who are on their own. He tracked me here. Thanks to you he didn't get me."

"Thanks to me and my throwing arm." Patty kissed her right bicep and whispered to it. "You rock."

"Anyway, that's the short version," Goldilocks said. "I'm in the woods because I'm on a case…and there's a lot on the line."

"That settles it then," Patty said.

"Settles what?"

"Tomorrow we find the grandparents' house so you can get back to work."

"We?" Goldilocks asked. "You're joining the case?"

"No, that's your job. But I can help you find the house. No one knows this forest like I do."

Goldilocks snorted. "No one but spiders and bears."

The two girls stretched out near the fire as it popped and sputtered, burning down to coals. Patty tossed Goldilocks a blanket and grabbed one for herself.

"Wow," Goldilocks said. "You're well supplied."

"I didn't leave the orphanage empty handed. Grabbed a few things before I left. I even have waterproof matches." She grimaced. "But try swimming a moat sometime without getting your backpack wet."

"Doesn't sound easy," Goldilocks said. Then she yawned and pulled the blanket to her chin. "Thanks again for the rescue, Patty Wagon Patty."

"You're welcome, Goldilocks the private eye."

The next morning Goldilocks woke to the sound of a crackling fire. She sat up, keeping the blanket over her shoulders. "I thought you didn't have a fire during the day."

"I don't, not usually. But I have a guest who's on a mission and needs her strength." Patty gestured toward the fire where something was roasting.

The morning light revealed that Patty's hair was indeed red. "You have red hair," Goldilocks said.

"I do," Patty replied. "Ever had rabbit?"

"You caught a rabbit? What did you do, hit it with a rock?"

Patty shook her head. "I'm good, but not that good. No, I checked my traps this morning while you were sleeping."

"You have traps?" Goldilocks eyes widened. "What are you, some kind of mountain woman?"

"Just a girl," Patty said. "But I used to be a Girl Scout. I know things."

Including how to cook.

"Not bad," Goldilocks said a few minutes later as she took a bite of rabbit.

They ate quickly. Then Patty kicked out the fire. "Now to find that house," she said with a smile. "I've never assisted a real detective before.

This might be fun."

"I just hope we're not eaten by bears," Goldilocks said. "Because that would—"

"Ruin your whole day?"

"Pretty much."

Goldilocks wandered back to a table made from a giant slab of bark suspended between two boulders. On it were seven baseball caps. "One for every day of the week?" Goldilocks asked.

Patty looked up from the fire, which she was still stomping on. "What's that?"

"Seven baseball caps," Goldilocks said, "for the seven days of the week?"

"I like variety," Patty said. "If I'm throwing too many balls, I change my hat. Helps me zone in on the strike zone, you know?"

"Changing your hat does all that?"

"Sometimes."

Goldilocks held up two of the caps. "Mind if I borrow a couple?"

"Sure, but what for?"

"Part of my uniform," Goldilocks explained. "Helps me zone in on clues. Helps me solve a mystery." Not that she had ever solved a mystery before, but it sure sounded good.

Chapter 12

A Walk in the Woods

It was still the Black Forest. Sunlight still didn't reach the forest floor. But somehow it was brighter and less scary, because Goldilocks, the private detective, the girl on a case, was no longer alone. Patty Wagon Patty seemed to know where she was going, and Goldilocks felt confident that with any luck, they'd find the yellow house with the white trim.

Solving the case might be a little trickier, but she'd worry about that when the time came. For now, she followed Patty and trusted she knew the way.

"You do know the way, right Patty?" Goldilocks asked after a while, just to be sure.

Patty shrugged. "You said the house is on the path, right?"

"Right."

"Well, I know the way to the path."

That was good enough for Goldilocks. Once they found the path, locating the house would be easy. The problem was the bears. Didn't bears have claws? And huge teeth? They might not take kindly to a little girl poking around.

"About those bears," Goldilocks said, thinking out loud.

Patty stopped beneath a tree with hanging vines. "What about them?"

"They're bears. If they know something about the missing grandparents, how do I get them to tell me? I don't speak bear. What am I supposed to do, growl at them?"

"Hmm," Patty said. She scratched her chin and thought it over. "You said the bears are living in the house, right?"

"Uh-huh."

"If they live like people, maybe they can talk like people." Patty lifted her shoulders and let them fall. "Maybe."

"Maybe they ate the grandparents," Goldilocks said in a worried voice. She walked forward, imagining the whole grizzly scene. Then she turned around and faced Patty. "They might think we're dessert."

"Goldilocks?"

"What?"

Patty pointed. "Don't. Move."

"What do you mean?" Goldilocks turned around again and walked right into a huge spider web. Her first instinct was to panic. Hands and feet shaking at once—it was an all-out-I'm-stuck-in-a-spider-web dance. It went on for some time, complete with spins and twirls, until she remembered the day before. She stopped dancing. *It's just spider web goo*, she told herself. *There are no giant spiders in the Black Forest. It's just a bedtime story.*

But a second later, there was Patty, hacking at the spider web with a stick. Then she grabbed Goldilocks' hand. "It's time to go, Goldilocks. We've got to get out of here."

"I thought you said it was just a bedtime story."

"I did," Patty said. "But this bedtime story just happens to be true."

"What!"

"Look!" Patty pointed above them, where a spider, the size of a cat, was descending on a silky thread. "Run!"

More spiders descended from other trees. It was a spider family...or maybe a spider school. The two girls tore across the forest floor, dodging tree trunks and ducking hanging vines, behind them no less than a dozen giant spiders in pursuit.

"I hate true bedtime stories," Goldilocks panted. "Give me a non-true one any day."

"Save your breath."

"I think they're gaining."

"I said don't talk."

And in all the running, they ran right across the path.

Goldilocks looked over her shoulder. "Wasn't that the path?"

"It was," Patty replied, "but do you really want to stop now?"

Good point. Stopping now meant becoming spider food. And so they kept going, blazing a trail through the ferns and low bushes of the Black Forest.

After a while, Goldilocks looked back. "I think we're pulling away."

"Yeah, but look." Patty stopped suddenly and grabbed onto Goldilocks. They'd come to the edge of a steep cliff overlooking a river. It was too wide to jump across. Behind them, the spiders kept coming.

Goldilocks swallowed hard, gazing down at the white water. "Guess we don't have a choice. We're breakfast if we stay here. How are your swimming skills, Patty?"

"My swimming skills are fine. It's my jumping skills that are a little rusty."

But as Goldilocks had said, they didn't have a choice. It was jump or be eaten.

Goldilocks cinched the straps of her backpack. "Not a difficult decision. See you down river." And then she leapt from the cliff's edge, aiming for the deepest part of the river below.

A split second later she hit the water and was swept away.

Chapter 13
Wet Detective

Imagine shrinking yourself to the size of a hotdog and then jumping into a washing machine while it's running…on the cold cycle. One second you're upright, the next you're not. One second you're at the surface, the next your face is being dragged along the bottom.

This was Goldilocks' experience in the white water rapids below the cliff's edge—like body surfing in the ocean and having the wave break on top of you. Then breaking again and again.

Goldilocks gasped for breath and was dragged under. Up and down and sideways. Over and over and over. Churning like she was in a washing machine.

Until, suddenly the churning stopped. The river flattened out, the water smooth and gentle. Goldilocks bobbed to the surface and stayed there. She swam to the edge and crawled out onto a sandy beach. Only then did she think of Patty Wagon Patty. Did Patty follow her into the river, did she make the jump, or did the spiders get to her before she had a chance?

Goldilocks cupped her hands around her mouth and yelled, "Patty! Patty! Pat—"

And that's when she glimpsed the red hair coming through the white water upstream. The red hair surfaced then vanished, surfaced and vanished, until it hit the slow water and stayed up.

"Over here," Goldilocks called out.

Patty swam over and pulled herself onto the bank.

"Your jumping skills weren't that rusty after all," Goldilocks said, shaking out her curls, which weren't all that curly at the moment.

"It's not like I had a choice." Patty looked at her friend and smiled. "And you were fearless, no hesitation at all. Where'd that come from?"

"I hate spiders," Goldilocks said with a shiver. "I really, really hate spiders. Especially the kind that eat people." She gave her curls another shake. "So what do we do now?"

"What do we do now?" Patty asked. "The mission is still on, my friend. We find the path that leads to the house, and then Goldilocks Private Eye goes to work. You just escaped man-eating spiders and jumped from a cliff with no hesitation. A girl like that can handle bears."

"You really think so?"

"I'm not sure. But it was a pretty good pep talk, don't you think?"

Pep talk or no pep talk, the two girls were not only far from the path, they were wet and freezing.

"Please tell me you have those waterproof matches," Goldilocks said.

Patty reached into her pocket and pulled a wad of wooden matches wrapped in a rubber band. "Never leave home without them. What do you say we dry out and make plans?"

"I say yes."

In no time at all Patty had a fire going at the river's edge. It cracked and popped, sending up a plume of smoke.

"Oh, that's good," Goldilocks said, moving as close as she could without getting singed. "Bless you and your matches."

"Like I said, I never leave home without them. Girl Scouts are always prepared."

Goldilocks added a log to the fire. "Well, you girl scout types rock is all I'm saying." She unpacked her backpack and placed the items close to the fire—the trench coat, the ball caps, she fanned the pages of *The Wind in the Willows*.

"The Wind in the Willows?" Patty raised an eyebrow. "One of your detective tools?"

"My dad's favorite book. He used to read it to me when I was little. I returned the favor when he got sick." Goldilocks fanned the pages again. "Sentimental value, I guess. Like carrying around a piece of him."

"A piece of him? That's gross!"

"You know what I mean."

Patty nodded. "Yes, I do. If I knew who my dad was, I'd keep some kind of memento nearby."

"Exactly," Goldilocks said.

With their thorough soaking in the river, it was a good hour in front of the hot fire before they could even think of moving on. Plenty of time to talk. Goldilocks cleared her throat and asked the question she'd been pondering all day.

"So Patty, why do you live in the Black Forest? I mean of all places? You said living on the streets was pretty easy." Goldilocks gestured at the trees around them. "Why live here?"

"Why?"

Goldilocks nodded.

"Tom the Kid-Snatcher, that's why. The Orphanage Just Outside of Lick Skillet, that's why. You have no idea, Goldilocks—it really is a horrible place. It needs to be shut down.

"So the Black Forest it is. For now. And it's not like I never go into town."

"You mean to get the day-old bread?" Goldilocks asked.

"Yes, day-old bread, dented canned food that the market throws out, general trash picking. You wouldn't believe what you can find in the trash. Knives, rope, comic books. Are you a Green Lantern fan?"

"Kind of," Goldilocks admitted.

"Anyway, the point is—it's safer for me here, giant spiders and all. Tom the Kid-Snatcher stays away from the Black Forest."

"What do you mean?" Goldilocks said. "He chased me into the forest."

"He chased you because he saw you enter. He doesn't know I'm here." Patty gazed across the fire at her friend. "Hey, your curls are coming back."

Goldilocks felt her clothes. "I'm feeling pretty dry, too. Want to go?"

"Yeah," Patty said, getting to her feet. "Let's go talk to some bears."

Chapter 14

The Yellow House With the White Trim

Goldilocks shook out *The Wind in the Willows* and stuffed it in her backpack. Then she folded the trench coat and added the ball caps. She glanced up at Patty. "You're going to help with the investigation? I thought you were just going to help me find the house, and then ditch me."

"Yeah, that was the original plan," Patty admitted. "But that was before we experienced giant spiders and a raging river together."

Goldilocks laughed. "Feeling a bond, are you?"

"It's more than that, Goldilocks. Getting to know each other, you know? And missing grandparents replaced by bears? I'm curious. I have to see this thing through. Solve the mystery."

Goldilocks felt the same way. It was more than surviving giant spiders and raging rivers. Getting to know each other? Becoming friends? Why not solve a mystery together?

"Besides…" Patty trailed off.

"Besides what?"

"Besides, you have that I-need-an-assistant-to-solve-this-mystery look on your face."

Goldilocks put a hand to her cheeks and felt around as if it would tell her something. "I do?"

Patty nodded. "Kind of. So I'd like to tag along and help you solve this thing, if it's okay with you?"

"Are you kidding?" Goldilocks said. "Who wants to talk to bears alone?"

"Good. Besides, you might need somebody who knows how to throw things."

"That's true. I might."

Patty headed off the sand bank and into the trees. "The path is this way."

"You sure?"

"Pretty sure."

Patty led the way and Goldilocks followed. But now, as they moved away from the river and into the thick forest, everything had changed. The lightness Goldilocks had felt that morning because of the presence of her new friend and the thought that there was nothing dangerous in the Black Forest, was gone. There were dangerous things in the forest. Giant spiders, for one. Who knew what else?

Goldilocks found herself stopping often and scanning the trees above her, in case something decided to drop down on its silky thread. She also searched for spider webs. Now and again, she stopped and pointed. "Is that what I think it is?"

Patty nodded. "I see it," and diverted their path to avoid it.

This happened again and again, so it was a slow trek through the woods and a scary one. As Goldilocks had said, she really, really hated spiders. And man-eating spiders were the worst kind.

Several times she even thought of giving up the case. Too dangerous, she told herself, not worth the risk. But then she'd remember her cat. Charlotte was depending on her. And maybe, in her cat way, she believed in her.

For my cat, Goldilocks kept telling herself, forcing her feet to move forward one step at a time. *I'm doing this for Charlotte.*

They kept walking, weaving in and out of the trees, slipping over moss-covered logs and hopping a few small creeks.

And then, suddenly, there it was—the path.

"Which way?" Patty asked.

Goldilocks pointed. "Further in is my guess."

Patty gave her a confused look. "Further in?"

"Not toward town, in other words. Deeper into the forest. Further in."

Patty nodded and took the path to the right. Because of the thickness of the trees, the path meandered. It zigged and zagged. Still, a path was a path. It was much better than blazing their own trail.

And soon the path widened, the trees overhead opened. Sunlight poured in, revealing a small house in a clearing. It was a yellow house with white trim.

"Ta-da!" Patty gestured. "Goldilocks, I give you...the house."

"Shh!" Goldilocks said, crouching in the ferns at the edge of the clearing. "We're detectives on a case, Patty. Get down."

"Okay, Miss Detective," Patty whispered. "What's the plan?"

"We wait and watch." Goldilocks moved a fern aside and gazed at the house. It was two stories with a railed porch. There was a small lawn, which was overgrown, and there were wilted flowers up against the house.

No sign of life inside. No movement at all.

"What are we watching for?" Patty asked.

Goldilocks shrugged. "Bears, people, I don't know."

"I don't see anything."

"Yeah," Goldilocks said after a while. "No one's home. Time for plan B."

Patty shot her a look. "Plan B?"

"Breaking and entering." Goldilocks removed her backpack, pulled out the trench coat, and slipped it on. She rolled up the sleeves. Then she grabbed the baseball caps, putting one on backward and the other on forward.

"What are you doing?"

"Detective uniform," Goldilocks told her. "I'm on the job." She handed the magnifying glass to Patty. "Hold this and follow me."

Goldilocks sprinted across the lawn and up the porch steps. She knocked on the door. After several seconds, she knocked again.

No answer. She peered through a nearby window. Still no sign of life.

She went back to the door and was about knock a third time, when the door opened, and there was Patty, smiling away.

"How'd you get in?"

Patty jabbed a thumb over her shoulder. "A window was open in the back. I like this breaking and entering stuff. What do we do now?"

Goldilocks had no idea. This was her first case. But she'd seen plenty of detective movies.

"Give me the magnifying glass," Goldilocks said. "Time to look for clues." She stepped inside and closed the door. Then, grabbing the magnifying glass, she looked around. It was a tiny house and it was spotless. Unlike the overgrown lawn and the wilted flowers outside, the inside was tidy. No dust on the furniture in the living room and—

Patty sniffed. "Something's cooking."

"Don't get any ideas," Goldilocks said. "We're here to investigate, not eat."

"You're no fun," Patty grumbled.

Goldilocks crossed the living room and opened a door, revealing a set of stairs. "I'll check the basement, Patty. You check upstairs."

The basement. Gulp! Goldilocks thought. Weren't basements where all the bad stuff happened? She clicked on a light and headed down the steps, trying not to think about it. But how could she not? Monsters, murderers, spiders? It could be anything.

"Is…anybody…here?" she called out.

But all was quiet. And if there were any spiders at all, they were the tiny-house-in-the-woods variety. It was an ordinary basement, shelves full of paint cans and old tools, stacks of boxes, and a deep sink.

But no grandparents.

Goldilocks went back upstairs.

Patty was sitting on a chair in the living room, eating something out of a bowl.

"Patty, what are you doing?"

"This stuff is amazing. The best porridge I've ever tasted."

"We're supposed to be on a mission."

"I know. But my brain works better on a full stomach."

Goldilocks was about to protest, when her stomach rumbled. Come to think of it, she was kind of hungry. And they'd already broken and entered. What was a little food snitching?

Patty gestured toward the kitchen. "There's a few more bowls on the counter. You gotta try it."

Goldilocks went into the kitchen and saw two bowls. She grabbed a spoon and tasted the first one. "Aack!" she yelled, nearly dropping the spoon. It was way too hot.

She tried the other bowl. "Yuck!" She winced. It was too cold.

She went back to the living room, still holding the spoon. "May I?" she asked, dipping into Patty's bowl.

"Sure, take the rest. I'm full."

Goldilocks took a bite. It was just right. It was more than just right—it was the best porridge she'd ever tasted.

She took the bowl from Patty and sat down on a chair.

"Ouch!" she said, making a face.

"I know," Patty said. "Too hard."

Goldilocks stood up and tried another chair. It was so soft that she nearly disappeared into the cushions.

Patty stood up. "Try this one. It's perfect."

Goldilocks tried Patty's chair. It was perfect…it was just right.

"Told ya," Patty said.

Goldilocks finished the porridge and put the bowl back in the kitchen. "Time to check upstairs," she told Patty.

"Lead on," Patty said.

Goldilocks grabbed her magnifying glass and up she went.

Chapter 15

Tired Detectives

Upstairs was one huge bedroom. Goldilocks remembered the night before, sleeping on the ground by the fire. Here in front of her were three perfectly-made beds with colorful blankets and comforters. She was about to yawn but Patty beat her to it.

"I'm exhausted," Patty said. "I wouldn't mind catching forty winks." She went over to the smallest of the three beds and lay down. "Ahhhh, a real bed…take a load off, Goldilocks."

Goldilocks was about to protest. Weren't they on a case? Didn't they have to find the missing grandparents? Didn't she need to finish the job so she could get paid and pay the rent? Wasn't her cat counting on her?

The answer was yes, yes, yes, and yes. But she said nothing. Those beds looked comfortable, and the sight of Patty with her eyes closed… Goldilocks figured the case could wait. Besides, weren't you more alert after a short nap? Didn't your brain work more efficiently? And weren't efficient brains more likely to solve a case?

Goldilocks went over to one of the larger beds and lay down. Just like the chairs downstairs, this one was way too hard. She got up and tried the next one and soon found herself sinking into the mattress. Way too soft. She popped up again and walked over to the small bed.

"Move it over, Rover." she said to Patty.

Patty opened an eye. "I beg your pardon?"

"Those other beds are horrible. Mind if I join you?"

Patty scooted to the side. "Not at all."

"Just for a few minutes, right? Just a wink or two, then we'll get back to work."

That was the plan anyway, a few minutes of rest and then back to the case of the missing grandparents. But as soon as Goldilocks' head hit the pillow she fell fast asleep.

So did Patty Wagon Patty, snores and all.

Goldilocks' client was absolutely right. His grandparents were missing and bears were living in the yellow house with the white trim. Real live bears. The furry kind, the big teeth and claws variety. They just weren't home at the moment.

Earlier in the day, Mama Bear had made a huge pot of porridge, but it was so boiling hot that the bear family, which consisted of Papa Bear, Mama Bear, and Baby Bear, decided to take a long walk in the woods while the porridge cooled.

"I bet the porridge is cool by now," Papa Bear said in his huge Papa Bear voice.

"You're probably right," Mama Bear said in her Mama Bear voice.

"My feet hurt," Baby Bear said in his tiny Baby Bear voice.

And so the three bears returned to the yellow house with the white trim. As soon as they walked through the door, Papa Bear sensed something was not right. He smelled something and it wasn't porridge.

"Fe fi fo fum," he bellowed in his Papa Bear voice. "I smell the blood of—"

"Honey?" Mama Bear said, holding up a paw. "Wrong story."

"Oh, right." Papa Bear walked into the living room and said,

"Someone's been sitting in my chair."

Mama Bear said, "Someone's been sitting in my chair."

Baby Bear squeaked, "Someone's been sitting in my chair."

Papa Bear sniffed with his huge Papa-Bear-sized nose. "Definitely not porridge," he muttered. "Are you sure I can't say 'fe fi fo fum?'"

Mama Bear nodded. "Positive, Dear."

This was too bad. Papa Bear really felt like grinding someone's bones and making bread with it. Instead, he went into the kitchen. There on the counter were the three porridge bowls.

"Someone's been eating my porridge," Papa Bear said in his Papa Bear voice.

"Someone's been eating my porridge," his wife agreed.

"Someone's been eating my porridge," Baby Bear said. "And they ate it all up."

But there was no sign of the someone.

"Let's go upstairs," growled Papa Bear, feeling a little peeved and still feeling like grinding bones.

Up the stairs they went, Papa Bear followed by Mama and Baby. There before them stood the three beds, and once again the bear family had something to say on the matter.

"Someone's been sleeping in my bed," said Papa Bear.

"Someone's been sleeping in my bed," said Mama Bear.

Baby Bear pointed. "Someone's been sleeping in my bed and they're still there. Look, it's two someones!"

Goldilocks couldn't remember a time when she'd slept so soundly. As she lay in the small bed next to Patty Wagon Patty, she dreamt of her father. He was reading to her from the *Wind in the Willows* on a lazy afternoon, and all was well. She was safe and warm and happy.

Suddenly something got caught in her father's throat. He coughed and it came out like a growl. A big growl, like one made by a…bear. And he kept saying the word "bed" over and over. "Bed, bed, bed."

Goldilocks opened her eyes and sat up. There before her stood three bears, two huge ones and a small one.

"Wake up, Patty."

"What?" Patty said, sitting up and rubbing her eyes. She spotted the bears and screamed.

Goldilocks popped out of the bed. "Uh…I'm Goldilocks," she stammered. "Private eye…I'm on a case…missing grandparents…this is their house…uh…isn't it?" She was so flustered that the words came out in chunks.

Patty was already opening a window and climbing out onto the roof.

"Stop trying to explain, Goldilocks. They don't understand—they're bears. Run!"

Yes, they were bears. And who better to ask about the missing grandparents than the current occupants of the yellow house with the white trim, who just happened to be bears. This was what Goldilocks was thinking. The plan all along had been to talk to the bears. But now that she was standing right in front of them she could think of only one thing.

Run!

And that's exactly what she did. She ran to the window and dove out on the roof.

Chapter 16

On the Run...Again

"Run!" yelled Patty.

Really? Run? How far could they get? They were on a roof!

In any case, the two girls headed to the roof's edge and jumped into the branches of a nearby tree. Then they climbed down and sprinted into the woods. Goldilocks knew how it worked. Whoever was behind got eaten first. And so she pulled ahead of Patty Wagon Patty.

She tore through the ferns on the forest floor, Patty bringing up the rear.

Patty also knew how things worked. She was behind which meant she was closer to huge claws and sharp teeth. And bears, who hadn't had their porridge and who were probably very hungry.

And so she pulled ahead of Goldilocks. They went back and forth this way. First Goldilocks took the lead, then Patty did. Goldilocks, then Patty—on and on.

Deeper into the forest they ran, leaving the path far behind. Nothing but the denseness of the Black Forest closing in on every side.

After a while, they slowed to a stop. Goldilocks looked back. No sign of the bears. She bent over to catch her breath and looked up at Patty, panting. "First spiders and now bears. I really hate this job."

Patty shrugged. "We already knew there'd be bears."

"Yeah, but knowing about them and seeing them are two different things. And by the way, you were the one who screamed."

"I couldn't help myself. One minute I was dreaming pleasant dreams and the next..." she trailed off. Patty leaned against a fallen tree and shook her head." I didn't know they'd be so scary."

"I know," Goldilocks said. "Now that I've seen the bears." A single tear trickled down her cheek. She wiped it away.

Patty looked at Goldilocks, waiting for her to finish. "Now that you've seen the bears? Go on."

Goldilocks wiped at another tear. "This case in unsolvable, Patty. I miss my cat. I want to go home and see my cat. I'll wait for another case."

"But what if there are no more cases. You'll be thrown out into the street."

"Yeah," Goldilocks said, kicking at a fern. "Yeah." She and Charlotte tossed out onto the streets, scavenging through trashcans for food. But what else could she do?

The more they talked about it, the more Goldilocks realized that the case was over. And maybe her career as a private detective was also over. All she knew was she wanted to go home.

The question was how? There was no getting out of the forest without finding the path, and they had no idea where that was. A private detective with an unsolvable case and her assistant were lost in a forest full of bears and giant spiders.

"Any idea where the path is?" Goldilocks asked.

Patty was about to answer when—

Crack!

Was something coming their way, or did a branch just feel like cracking all by itself?

Patty stepped away from the log she'd been leaning on. "What was that?"

More twigs snapped. Something was coming their way. Goldilocks looked down at her legs and feet, hoping they had more to give, her heartbeat kicking into high gear. "Run, Patty. Run like you you've never run—"

"Wait!" said a tiny voice.

They were right. Something was coming their way, but it was a rather small something. It was Baby Bear.

She stood onto her hind legs, and looking at Goldilocks, said, "You're a private detective? Is that true?"

"It is," said Goldilocks, feeling her heartbeat slowing down again.

"And I'm her assistant," said Patty proudly.

"I love mysteries," said Baby Bear. "Can I help?"

Goldilocks made a face. "Help?"

"Yeah, help you solve the case. I'm a very logical bear. I can gather evidence, put two and two together. And I have a terrific nose. Besides, you have that look on your face."

"What look?" Goldilocks asked.

"That I-need-another-assistant-to-solve-this-case look." Baby Bear glanced at Patty. "Don't you think she has that look?"

"You kind of do, Goldilocks," Patty agreed.

"Hmmm." Goldilocks thought it over. A talking bear wanted to help her solve the case? A bear? She probably couldn't even hold a magnifying glass. "I don't know," she said. "Who ever heard of a detective with two assistants?"

Patty folded her arms, thinking. Then she pointed toward Baby Bear. "A creature who lives in the woods, helping us solve a case in the woods? Might be just what we need. Besides, she lives in the yellow house with the white trim."

"I do," Baby Bear agreed. "Did you say something about missing grandparents?"

"Yes," Goldilocks said. "They're missing and you're living in their house. What do you have to say about that?"

"I'm just a kid," Baby Bear said. "I live where my mom and dad tell me to live. I don't know what happened to any grandparents, but I bet my parents do."

This was one logical bear. She really did know how to put two and two together. Maybe Goldilocks could use another assistant. Maybe the best way to interview the bears (the big bears) was to have the little bear do the talking.

"You're hired," Goldilocks said. "Let's go talk to your mom and dad."

That was the plan anyway, go talk to the bears and let the smallest member of the family conduct the interview. But before Goldilocks could take a step, there was a swishing sound and a long piece of rope, weighted on each end, wrapped around her ankles, tossing her to the ground.

"Don't anybody move!"

It was Tom the Kid-Snatcher. He was swinging another length of rope over his head like he was some kind of demented cowboy. "Yee-ha!" he yelled. A second later he let it fly, and down went Patty Wagon Patty.

Tom the Kid-Snatcher stood thirty yards away. "Wrapped up and neatly packaged," he said with a smile, which was more smirk than smile. "Life is good, isn't it? Sometimes it just hits you. How good life is. Here I was looking for the girl with the golden hair and I got the escapee to boot. Two for one. How about that?"

He threw his head back and laughed. Then he glanced at Baby Bear and said, "I don't have any use for a bear, though. Get along, little fella. Shoo! Scat!"

Baby didn't move at all. Her snout was working overtime, sniffing. Something was coming their way, and it made her smile. She looked up at Tom the Kid-Snatcher and said, "You might want to leave now, sir."

"What?" Tom the Kid-Snatcher was dumbfounded. A talking bear? And a polite one at that. Was he imagining things?

If he was, he was about to imagine it again.

"My mom and dad are coming, Sir," Baby Bear said. "You don't want to be here when they arrive."

"What?" Tom said again. Leave his captives? After all he'd been through? Nothing doing. Not on your life.

And then—

A roar!

A rather mighty roar blasted through the forest. And there was Papa Bear, moving through the brush. He reared up onto his hind legs and roared again. A second later, Mama Bear appeared, adding her roar to her husband's. It wasn't as mighty, but it was close.

Goldilocks sat up and began untying herself.

Papa bear dropped to all fours and sauntered over. "Relax, kid," he whispered to Goldilocks. "I'll take care of the hairy guy," meaning Tom the Kid-Snatcher.

"Wait!" Goldilocks whispered back. She had an idea. "Drag me into the woods."

Papa Bear grimaced. "What?"

"Drag me into the woods," Goldilocks whispered again. "He'll never come after me again if he thinks I'm dead. He'll give up the chase for good."

Patty sat up and whispered. "What are you saying?"

"Trust me," Goldilocks said. "This is the only way. Drag me into the woods." She looked up at Mama Bear, then nodded toward Patty. "Drag her. Make it look real."

Papa Bear stood on his hind legs and roared louder than before. Mama Bear did the same. Then they dropped to all fours and grabbed Goldilocks and Patty and dragged them into the woods—deep into the Black Forest.

"No, no," Goldilocks screamed. *"Nooooooo—"*

And then she went quiet and so did Patty.

Gone. Devoured by bears.

Tom the Kid-Snatcher was left standing alone in the woods, thankful to be alive but without the two captives he had hoped for.

The director of The Orphanage Just Outside of Lick Skillet would not be happy.

Chapter 17

The Case of the Missing Grandparents

"Okay, that's enough dragging," Goldilocks said.

Papa Bear didn't hear. He was too busy dragging, too busy making it look real. Meanwhile, Goldilocks head was thumping along on the rough forest floor.

"I SAID THAT'S ENOUGH DRAGGING!" Goldilocks yelled at the top of her lungs.

Papa Bear let go and Mama Bear did the same. A few seconds later Baby Bear pulled up.

"Mom, Dad," she began. "What happened to the grandparents?" She gestured toward Goldilocks and Patty. "These guys are real detectives... and I'm their new spokesperson."

In fact, she was a spokesbear.

Mama Bear and Papa Bear exchanged a look.

"What happened to them?" Baby Bear asked again.

Papa looked through the trees. Not far away stood the yellow house with the white trim. "There's porridge in there with my name on it. Who's hungry?"

Everyone raised a hand, including Goldilocks and Patty. They weren't really all that hungry. They were just stressed from almost being captured by Tom the Kid-Snatcher and from being fake-devoured by bears. More porridge might do the two detectives good.

Papa Bear led the way. "Let's go eat and talk it over."

Papa Bear belched loudly and pushed his bowl away.

"Honey!" Mama Bear gave her husband a disapproving look. "We have guests."

"I know that, but I'm a bear."

Just to make him feel better, Goldilocks forced a burp of her own. For a small girl she really knew how to burp. Kind of like a lumberjack...or a truck driver. She pushed her bowl away and looked up at Papa Bear. "What can you tell us about the missing grandparents?" she asked.

"What can I tell you?"

"Yes."

Papa Bear huffed. "I can tell you they're not missing, that's what I can tell you."

"What do you mean?" Patty asked. "Where are they?"

"Can't people go on vacation around here without everyone getting suspicious? They left for Fort Lauderdale and asked us to housesit for them. We accepted." Papa Bear gestured around. "This is way better than our den."

"Plus, we get to eat porridge, Papa," Baby Bear added. She looked at Goldilocks and Patty. "And we have cable."

Goldilocks and Patty exchanged a look. Then they both burst out laughing.

"Wow," Goldilocks said. "And all this time we thought they were bear food."

"Bear food?" Mama Bear shook her head. "We're not that kind of bear."

Thank goodness, Goldilocks said to herself. Then she smiled. Things were looking up. The grandparents were on vacation. She'd relay the information to her client, collect her fee, pay the rent, and feed her cat.

It had been a while since Charlotte had eaten. Goldilocks needed to get home and get there quickly. She glanced at Mama and Papa Bear. "Do you have their address?"

"Of course," said Papa Bear. He handed her a piece of paper, which had the travel information.

The two girls thanked the bears and headed for the door.

"If you ever need help on a another case," Baby Bear pointed at her chest, "I'm your bear."

"Absolutely," Goldilocks said. "You're the best bear detective I know."

Goldilocks and Patty headed down the path, which led out of the Black Forest. But now that Tom the Kid-Snatcher thought they had been devoured by bears, they had to be careful not to be seen.

But Goldilocks didn't want to think about Tom the Kid-Snatcher. She had solved the case. The grandparents were alive and well. She'd be able to pay the rent and not get tossed into the street.

She glanced at Patty and said, "So how'd you like working the case?"

"I loved it," Patty said.

"I could use a good assistant. And my apartment has two bedrooms."

Goldilocks flashed on how quickly she had drifted off to sleep in Baby

Bear's bed, how good it had felt after sleeping next to the fire the night before. "Two comfortable beds. After all, you do have that look on your face."

"What look?"

"That I'm-tired-of-sleeping-on-the-ground-and-would-much-prefer-a-bed look on your face."

"I do?"

"Absolutely. Want to be roommates?"

Patty thought for a moment, then shook her head. "Do you think I'm a softy? I live off the land. I trap rabbits and live in a cave."

"That's not what the look on your face is saying," Goldilocks said.

"Looks can be deceiving, Goldilocks."

"Are you sure?"

"Pretty sure."

Goldilocks nodded. It was worth a try. "Suit yourself. It was just an idea."

When the two girls reached the edge of the Black Forest, they parted ways, Goldilocks heading toward Lick Skillet, and Patty Wagon Patty heading for her place in the woods.

"Be safe," Goldilocks called to her.

"You too," Patty said.

Goldilocks met up with her thin-mustached client at the Café de Grub. They sipped milkshakes while Goldilocks relayed the information of the so-called missing grandparents.

"Fort Lauderdale?" the client said.

"Fort Lauderdale," Goldilocks said, and she slid the piece of paper at him with the hotel's address and phone number.

The client smiled. Then he pulled an envelope from his jacket pocket and handed it to Goldilocks. "Worth every penny. Thank you."

"Thank you," she said. She pushed her milkshake aside and left the Café de Grub. She couldn't wait to see Charlotte and tell her all about her adventures. The spiders, the bears, Patty Wagon Patty—it had been a very busy couple of days.

But then, just outside the café, she ran into her least favorite person on the entire planet.

It was Tom the Kid-Snatcher, and he didn't look happy.

Chapter 18

Tom the Kid-Snatcher

Well, she didn't actually run into him.

But she saw him—just half a block away. Fortunately, he hadn't spotted her. Not yet. *Think*, Goldilocks said to herself. *Hide—but where?*

She had no time to think. And even less time to hide. So she did the only thing she could do. She got off the street—ASAP—grabbing for the nearest door along Main Street and rushing inside.

It was a salon. Manicures, pedicures, hairdressing. Goldilocks dashed for one of the empty chairs and pulled a hairdryer down over her head.

"Can I help you, young lady?" the owner of the salon asked.

"Uh…" came Goldilocks' muffled voice, "can I stay under this thing for a couple of hours? It's very comfortable." As hiding places go, under a hairdryer in a salon was a pretty good one. All you could see were torso and legs.

"I'm afraid not," said the salon owner. She was a skinny lady with dark hair and large hoop earrings. Other than Goldilocks and herself, the salon was empty.

Goldilocks peeked out from under the hairdryer. "No?"

"No," the salon owner said. "We don't play hide and seek here. We cut and color hair."

This gave Goldilocks an idea. She glanced at the photos on the salon walls, all sorts of hairstyles in all sorts of colors. "Okay, hair cut it is. Hack off these curls and dye what's left dark brown."

The salon lady nodded. "You got it."

In the next half hour, the girl with the golden curls known as Goldilocks became something very un-goldenlocked. When the salon lady was finished, there were no curls at all, and what was left was anything but golden.

"Why, you look like a brand new person," the salon lady said with a smile.

"Works for me," Goldilocks said, jumping to her feet. She went to the door and looked out. Tom the Kid-Snatcher was still there, sitting on the Patty Wagon, smoking a cigarette.

Should she risk it? Tom the Kid-Snatcher probably wouldn't recognize her, but just the same, he was a kid-snatcher. Wouldn't he be just as happy to grab a dark-haired girl as one with flowing locks?

Goldilocks turned to the salon lady. "How'd you like to earn a fast fifty bucks?"

"I beg your pardon?" said the salon lady.

"It'll be easy money. Trust me."

A few minutes later, Goldilocks, who now had short brown hair, was walking down Main Street, hand in hand with the salon lady. They strolled right past Tom the Kid-Snatcher in broad daylight.

"Top of the morning to you," Goldilocks said to him with a smile, even though it was now late afternoon. "Nice weather we're having."

Tom the Kid-Snatcher said nothing. He glared and scowled. You would too if you'd lost the golden-haired girl and Patty Wagon Patty all in the same day. Maybe that's why he was loitering in town. He couldn't bear to return to The Orphanage Just Outside of Lick Skillet empty handed. He also couldn't bear to face the orphanage director.

Goldilocks and the salon lady sauntered on, stopping only once to buy cat food and a few other things. When they reached the apartment building, Goldilocks paid the salon lady and thanked her for her excellent acting job, then she knocked on the landlady's door.

"It's me, Mrs. Vanderflip," she called. "It's Goldilocks."

The door opened and there stood Mrs. Vanderflip, still in her tool belt, gray hair stuffed beneath her ball cap. "Goldilocks?" she said. "You don't look like Goldilocks."

"New hairdo," Goldilocks said. Then she reached into her pocket and handed her the rent money, three months worth. "I told you I had a plan."

Mrs. Vanderflip held the rent money like she was seeing things, like she'd wake up any minute.

"It's real, Mrs. Vanderflip. You're not dreaming. Want me to pinch you?"

Mrs. Vanderflip didn't reply, and Goldilocks didn't feel like sticking around to talk it over. She had a cat to feed. She dashed up the stairs and into her apartment/office.

"It's me, Charlotte. I'm home."

It took a while for Charlotte to come around. After all, she was used to sharing the apartment with a girl with golden curls. Who was this dark-haired variety? And where were the golden curls?

It was the food that won her over. Once Goldilocks opened the can of cat food, Charlotte recognized her. The same food, the same voice…it had to be the same girl. Charlotte rubbed against Goldilocks' ankles and purred.

"It nice to see you too, Charlotte," Goldilocks said. She reached down to pet her. Then she made herself a peanut butter and banana sandwich and sat in the kitchen with her cat.

When their stomachs were full, they went into the living room and watched the sun go down. "It's nice to be home, Charlotte," Goldilocks told her.

Yes, it was very nice—no giant spiders to worry about, and once again, she'd given Tom the Kid-Snatcher the slip.

Goldilocks grabbed the remote and turned on the television. It was her favorite show, about a dog detective and his cat assistant. Together they solved mysteries and fought crime in New York City. Drug dealers, bank robbers, jewel thieves—they did it all. And now that she was a mystery solver and crime fighter herself, Goldilocks watched with renewed interest.

She watched two episodes, back to back—it was a Dog and Cat Detective marathon. She was halfway into a third show, when there was a knock on the door.

Goldilocks nearly jumped out of her seat.

Uh-oh! Maybe her disguise hadn't fooled Tom the Kid-Snatcher. After all she'd been through, to be captured now? It was unthinkable.

"Charlotte, what do I do?"

Meow!

"Jump out the window? Are you serious? We're on the second floor!"

The knock came again.

Goldilocks' heart raced. She crept to the peephole and looked out. Then she opened the door.

It was Patty Wagon Patty. She held up a bakery bag, then let her hand drop. "Uh…isn't this the Goldilocks Detective Agency?"

"It's me, Patty," Goldilocks said. "New disguise."

Patty's took a step forward and squinted. Then her face broke into a smile. She held up the bag again. "So it is. Can I come in? I've got rolls."

Goldilocks let Patty in and closed the door behind her.

"So you've rethought my offer?" Goldilocks asked.

"Why, do I have that I'm-tired-of-the-woods-and-would-like-to-sleep-in-a-real-bed look on my face?"

Goldilocks nodded and reached for a roll. "You kind of do."

"Yes," Patty said, "but it's more than that." She looked Goldilocks in the eye. "How are you at writing letters?"

Chapter 19

The Goldilocks Detective Agency

"I got an A in English," Goldilocks said proudly. "I know what a sentence is. Why? What kind of letter?"

Patty sat down on the couch. "Remember what I said about The Orphanage Just Outside of Lick Skillet?"

"Uh-huh…rats and cockroaches?"

"It's gotten worse," Patty said. "Now they've added corporal punishment."

"Corporal *what*ishment?"

"You know, spankings, beatings. It used to be just drafty buildings, rodents, and bugs. Now they're hitting the kids."

"How do you know?" Goldilocks asked. "You've been living in the woods for quite a while."

"I snuck into town tonight after the sun went down to check out the day-old bread." She held up the roll she'd been chewing on. "Rolls, you know? Anyway, I bumped into Henry from the orphanage."

"Henry Wagon Henry?"

"Yes, he escaped the same way I did…climbed over the wall, swam the moat. He told me about Tom the Kid-Snatcher losing it completely. Spanking all the kids for no reason at all. Just because he felt like it."

Goldilocks nodded. "We gotta do something."

"Exactly. Grab some paper and a pen, Goldilocks. It's time to alert the authorities."

To the Department of Child Services…

To Whom it May Concern:
This is to inform you of the horrendous living conditions of The Orphanage Just Outside of Lick Skillet and the deviant behavior of certain staff members….

Goldilocks put down her pen and looked up at Patty. "How's that for a beginning?"

"Perfect," Patty said. "Tell them about the rats, the cockroaches, the mass beatings."

Goldilocks did, and then some. Everything spelled out in black and white, even though the ink was blue. When she finished, both girls signed the letter.

"That should do it," Patty said, sealing the envelope.

"It should," Goldilocks agreed. "Here's hoping they'll lock up Tom the Kid-Snatcher for a very long time." She flicked her short hair. "And when they do, I'm growing my golden curls back."

"I miss those curls," Patty said. "You'd have to change the name of your business otherwise."

"I know. And the Goldilocks Detective Agency has already solved a case. We can't change the name now." Goldilocks stood up from the desk, where she'd been writing the letter. "How about omelets for dinner?"

"I'm in," Patty said.

And so omelets it was...with bacon and cheese. The two girls sat down to their feast. Goldilocks looked across the table at her friend and smiled.

"What? Do I still have that look on my face?" Patty asked.

"You do," Goldilocks said.

"That I-want-to-sleep-in-a-bed-tonight look?"

"The I-want-to-be-partners-in-a-detective-agency look," Goldilocks said. But she knew it was much more than that. It was more than a bed to sleep in and more than a detective agency. It was about a friendship, a sisterhood…girl power. It was about a future that neither of them could predict.

And isn't that the way it should be?

The next morning, the girls woke to the sound of a knock on the door.

Oh no! Goldilocks sat up, rubbing her eyes. *It's Tom the Kid-Snatcher. The disguise didn't fool him at all!*

Goldilocks came out of the bedroom and saw Patty standing there in her nightgown.

"What do we do, Goldilocks?"

Meow.

"Climb out the window. Are you kidding me?" Goldilocks went up to the peephole, trying not fear the worst. How would they get away this time? And what about Charlotte?

But it wasn't Tom the Kid-Snatcher. It wasn't a man at all. It was a middle-aged woman, wringing her hands and looking rather distressed.

Goldilocks opened the door.

"Is this the Goldilocks Detective Agency?" the lady asked in a shaky voice.

"It is," Goldilocks said. "Come in."

The lady stepped inside. "I hear missing persons is your specialty."

"You heard right," Patty said. "Have a seat and tell us all about it."

The lady walked over to the desk and sat before it as Goldilocks grabbed a pad of paper and pen and sat on the other side.

"Go on," Goldilocks said.

"My niece and my nephew are missing," the lady said, still wringing her hands. "I'm worried sick about them."

She looks worried sick, Patty thought. Or at least she looked sick, which was a start.

Goldilocks nodded, jotting it down on her notepad. Then she looked up. "This niece and nephew of yours—what are their names?"

"Hansel and Gretel," the lady said. "I need you to find them and bring them home. Can you do that? Will you take the case?"

The two girls exchanged a look. "Absolutely!" they said in unison.

After all, some people were missing and Goldilocks and her new assistant were missing-people-finders. Their last case was a success. They located the missing grandparents. They survived spiders, bears, and a wild-haired man. Certainly they could find a couple of lost kids.

Goldilocks looked up from her notepad. "Tell us more," she said.

"Yes," Patty said, "tell us all about Hansel and Gretel."

BOOKS BY GREG TRINE

Melvin Beederman Superhero Series
The Curse of the Bologna Sandwich
The Revenge of the McNasty Brothers
The Grateful Fred
Terror in Tights
The Fake Cape Caper
Attack of the Valley Girls
The Brotherhood of the Traveling Underpants
Invasion from Planet Dork

The Second Base Club

The Adventures of Jo Schmo
Dinos Are Forever
Wyatt Burp Rides Again
Shifty Business
Pinkbeard's Revenge

Willy Maykit in Space

ABOUT THE AUTHOR

Greg is the author of the *Melvin Beederman Superhero Series*,
The Adventures of Jo Schmo, *Willy Maykit in Space*, and others.
He lives with his family in California.

www.gregtrine.com

ABOUT THE ILLUSTRATOR

Ira loves to illustrate books for children and has created twenty
children's books. She lives and works in Lviv, Ukraine.

www.baykovska.com

CPSIA information can be obtained
at www.ICGtesting.com
Printed in the USA
LVHW090207210919
631812LV00006B/13/P

9 781733 958929